A Courier for Christmas

Eliza Anne

To anyone who has ever wanted to be bent over your boss's desk by the delivery driver...
Merry Christmas.

Content Warning

- Whiplash

While not written into the story, if you've read previous Eliza Anne books, this short story will figuratively give you whiplash. This is a funny, smutty romantic comedy. Trauma is nearly nonexistent in this one. Unless the thought of destroyed books makes you cry, there is no emotional damage.

*Please note that A Courier for Christmas has explicit on page sex scenes and other mature adult content.

Chapter 1

Jules

29 Days 'til—

"Liv, I don't even have the boxes unpacked. There's no reason to be putting up a letterboard reminder." I slide another tote across the floor with a huff. We arrived at my new apartment in Coals Lake three hours ago. My couch is in the middle of my living room and every single thing I own is stacked in the foyer. The moving company was a little too eager to get my things unloaded and leave. "Can you help with this?"

My best friend turns from the board to view the array of boxes spread throughout the room and scrunches her face. "Hmmm, I don't know. Those look heavy."

"Seriously?" I balk. Reaching for the closest thing I can throw at her, I grab the pillow from the corner of the couch.

Liv smirks, places the plastic tray of letters on the dining room table beside a tower of more shit, and holds her hands up in surrender. "I'm kidding. I'm kidding."

"Ya know, if you were the eighth dwarf, you'd be Pesky," I playfully chide.

"And if you were the ninth, you'd be Bitchy," Liv throws back without a single ounce of hesitation.

I join in on her laughter at the horrible banter and heft a tote of clothing. Walking from the room, I don't want to get sappy right now, I'll save that for the airport tomorrow, but I really will miss the hell out of her. Liv and I have been attached at the hip since birth; we've never lived so far apart.

It doesn't take long for us to get the boxes into their respective rooms, and once the living area is a bit more cleaned up, exhaustion starts to hit. Between finishing my final days of work in Oregon, packing, and moving to an entirely different country, this last week has been a hell of a whirlwind, and I find my body begging to slow down. Unfortunately, there's no time to rest, so caffeine will have to do. "Do you want to grab coffee before we do anything else? I'm tired."

"A thousand percent, yes." Liv perks up at my suggestion. Her brunette hair is splayed across the arm of the couch where she dramatically crashed once we managed to scoot it where I wanted.

"Perfect." After slipping on my shoes, I look around the space. "I think my keys are in the kitchen; I'll be right back." As I turn to retreat, there is a knock on the door.

Liv and I look at each other, both confused. "Who is that?"

"No idea," I shrug, stepping lightly across the hardwood and looking through the peephole. Whoever's standing there has a delivery company logo on his uniform that I recognize, but I can't make out much else. "Courier, I guess."

"I'll get your keys," Liv stands from her perch on the edge of my couch and walks to the kitchen.

Wrenching the door open, a shiver works its way through my bones as the cold air brushes my cheeks. "Can I help y—" The rest of the question is stolen from my throat as my eyes connect with the man in front of me. I'm not sure what I was expecting, but a six-foot-something Greek god on my doorstep was not it.

His dark-brown eyes are warm and inviting as he shifts a box beneath his arm. "Hey, I've got a package here that needs a signature." The driver holds out a digital pen and the device, but I'm too busy ogling to process what he's saying.

I swallow hard, suddenly regretting the stained sweats, and unwashed Christmas sweater I chose to wear today. My hair is thrown into the world's messiest bun and the bags under my eyes are a personality trait at this point. My mother would be aghast if she could see me right now.

Fuck.

For some reason, my hands seem to continue functioning even though my brain lags, and I grab the pen he's offering. A breeze brushes softly from behind him, and the cedarwood scent wafting through the air has me reeling.

"Got them!" Liv calls from behind me, pulling me out of whatever trance this statuesque delivery driver put me in.

"Oh, um…" I shake my head in confusion. "Is it for Jules Harrington?" I'm perplexed as to what would be getting delivered today, and suddenly realize that I shouldn't be signing for someone else. My own mother doesn't even know my address yet. He flips the box so the label is up and shakes his head. I step further into the cold, leaning forward, breathing in that euphoric scent, and reading a name I don't recognize. "That must be the old occupant; I just moved in today. I'm sorry."

I pass the pen back to him, and he returns it with the signature pad to his pocket. "Oh. No worries, then. Welcome to Coals Lake." The megawatt smile he offers alongside the northern hospitality has me damn near swooning all over again. "Have a good day, ladies." With a tip of his head, he retreats to his truck.

Lingering in the doorway longer than I should, Liv's voice is a jump scare when I realize she's moved to stand directly behind me.

"What's your address?" she asks. Before I can even answer she waves her hand in the air and answers her own question. "Oh, never mind. I can just look at your location."

"Why?"

"Don't worry about it." She begins typing as she speaks, and I know she's up to no good.

"What are you doing?" I view the shopping app over her shoulder and gasp. "Olivia! Jesus, I do not need a *personal massage device.*"

"I helped you pack, Jules. You don't own a single vibrator, and if the men here look like *that*, you're gonna need one." Her bright blue eyes are full of mischief when she slides her phone back in the pocket of her jeans and hands me my keys as she walks past, "It will be here tomorrow. If we're lucky, Delivery Daddy will stop by again."

I huff and rush to follow after her. "*Delivery Daddy?* For the love of—Liv. The man is probably married for all we know."

"He's not. I checked." Satisfied with herself, she pulls open the car door and settles in. When I join her, she continues, "I think it's okay to have some fun, Jules. You don't have to commit to anything. But as your best friend and self-appointed wing woman, sex would do you good."

I put the car in drive and pull out of the parking lot. "Damn, tell me how you really feel."

"What? It's been like a year, Jules. There's gotta be dust mites down there by now."

"Olivia!" She's nothing if not direct. "Yes. The courier was attractive, but can we drop it? I'm still recovering from Ty—"

"Oh, fuck that guy. His dick couldn't touch grass if it was hard and he was laying down."

The outburst throws me into another fit of laughter. I should have known the mention of his name would send her into a frenzy. She got a bit protective when he fucked me over. Still, there were no lies. Love was truly blind when it came to my relationship with him.

The cafe isn't far away, so we are already pulling into a parking space. I shut the car off and turn toward her. "Okay, okay. If the opportunity presents itself, I'll consider the delivery driver. But after seeing me looking like I crawled from beneath a bridge to collect a toll, I doubt he's interested."

"One, you're the hottest bridge troll I know." That elicits another giggle from me. She holds up a second finger, her eyes softening as she speaks this time. "Two, I want you to be happy. Even if it's not sex with the ridiculously attractive courier, just try opening yourself up again."

"Thanks, Liv." I lean across the console to give her a hug. She knows how hard it has been for me to even *think* of dating again, but maybe her point is valid. Happiness doesn't have to come from commitment.

Chapter 2

Samuel

I'm halfway through the day, and becoming increasingly frustrated with the way my loader threw these packages onto my truck. The longer it takes me to look for a stop, the longer my days are. I look at my driver helper, Paul, who is rummaging around in the front. "Find it yet?"

He's standing on his tiptoes, reaching for the edge of a long, small package in the back. "I think this is the one." His fingertips brush the corner, and it falls to the ground with a thud. "Shit." He reaches down to pick up the parcel, but the cardboard box slips from his fingers and falls to the ground once more. Watching him scoop the item up and drop it a third time has me shaking my head in exasperation. At this point, I just hope the contents aren't fragile because otherwise we're fucked.

"I got it, man." My gloves grip the package with ease. Flipping it to read the label and make sure this is the one I need, I grin. *Jules Harrington.* "No, fucking way." The words were only intended for myself, but Paul is directly behind me. *Why is he standing so close?*

"Huh?"

"Nothing. I'll take this. Can you run these to apartment 2C?"

"Sure thing, boss." Paul takes the three packages I'd already placed up front and scurries off.

I haven't forgotten Jules from yesterday. The way heat rose to her cheeks, and those blue eyes trailed my body. How she became so flustered at the sight of me was cute, and I walk with a bit more of a pep in my step at the thought of seeing her again.

Several minutes pass after I knock on her door, and I start to think she isn't home. Even though the item is a shipper release, I don't really want to leave it on her doorstep looking like Paul sent it through a garbage compactor. So, I pull my board out to list the package as damaged.

As I turn to leave, the lock clicks. "Sorry, I was on the phone."

I don't even have to say anything. Her eyes immediately widen at the sight of me, and   a pink hue creeps up her cheeks. *There it is.* When she notices the package in my hand, her face falls. I can't even blame her for being upset at the state it's in. "Oh my God."

"Things shift in the truck sometimes. It fell off the shelf. If you'd like to return it, I can—"

Unable to even finish my sentence, she snatches the box from my hand. Her haste causes her to fumble the cardboard package, and for the fourth time today, the poor thing takes another tumble to the ground. Only, this time, whatever she ordered immediately starts vibrating. Her cheeks turn crimson. Glancing at me in horror, she quickly picks it up and launches it across her living room like a damn hot potato. The faint sound of someone saying, "ow," meets my ears before raucous laughter.

I can't help but find humor in the whole situation. "My *friend-*" Jules' face is still as bright as a stoplight as she glares at whoever is sitting across the room, still laughing. "Was here yesterday and thought that would be a funny joke after you—" Stopping herself, her eyes widen a nearly imperceptible amount, and she clears her throat. "Anyway, I don't need to return anything. Thank you."

By now, she's dropped her gaze to the ground, not even making eye contact with me, and I feel bad for how embarrassed she is.

"Ask him if he's single," her friend calls from across the room, no shame at all in her antics, and I can no longer hold in my laugh.

"Have a good day," Jules rushes out.

Before she closes the door all the way, I'm still chuckling when I follow with, "I am by the way." The door stops and I think she's going to say something else. But even though the confirmation made her falter, she ultimately closes it without any further conversation, and I'm left on her doorstep staring at the apartment number.

Twice now, I've found myself in humorous interactions with Jules Harrington, and I'd be lying if I said I wasn't hopeful for more. I realize my thoughts are so consumed that I forgot about Paul, who is more than likely freezing in the truck by now, so I pick up the pace. He's in his seat, patiently waiting when I slide the door open. "Sorry, man."

"It's all good." His damn teeth are chattering as he talks, and I hurry to get the heat back on.

He may be clumsy as hell, but the guy has got to be the nicest, most passive person I know. Though, for as much as I like him, he will be sitting in the truck every time Coals Lake's newest resident gets another package.

Chapter 3

Jules

"Liv, stop sending me shit. I look like I have an addiction." I squeeze the phone between my ear and shoulder, toss a bottle of chocolate syrup in my cart, and cross the topping off my list.

"It's not my fault all of your Christmas gifts were sent separately… on different days of the week," she feigns innocence. Although, I know her intentions are anything but. I've received over eight packages in the last five days, and coincidentally, it's been the same courier every time.

"You're meddling," I accuse, unwilling to admit I was a little upset that it's Sunday and I missed my daily dose of eye candy.

"I'm not meddling. I'm only getting you what you need."

"I didn't *need* a cat sweater," I deadpan.

"First off, that sweater was fucking cute," she gasps defensively. "Second, I wasn't talking about the sweater."

Heading to the dairy aisle, I roll my eyes. "I don't *need* the courier either."

"Just his number," she confirms.

I wish. "Stop meddling."

"Ugh, fine." There is no missing the disappointment in her voice as she concedes, and I'm not sure I believe she's giving up so easily.

"Anyway, I'm at the grocery store. I'll call you tonight. Love you."

She offers her goodbye, and I hang up. Grabbing the whipping cream, I toss the last item on my list into the cart. Why we are having an ice cream social at work tomorrow when the temperature is in the negatives is beyond me, but I will show up with a smile on my face and greet my new employees nonetheless.

The cashier is a sweet older woman, who instantly brings up that I must not be from around here. I've gotten that a lot this week. Coals Lake seems to be one of those towns where everybody knows everybody, and if they don't know you, they want to.

I have yet to meet anyone who wasn't accommodating, and I appreciate that. While I'm not used to the hospitality, it's a nice reprieve from city life.

Passing me my receipt, the talkative woman wishes me well and I head out the doors with my single sack of items. The cold has a bite to it today, making me shiver. I look around at the snow-covered pines, and salt-laden parking lot. I'm used to low-temperature winters, but this weather just seems different. Perhaps it has to do with the regional layout, or maybe it's   psychosomatic as I've only gone a bit further north in the move.

By the time I reach my car, I'm cursing myself for not wearing gloves. I shift the paper sack in my arms to retrieve the key from my coat pocket, but my fingers have already become stiff from the cold, and the bag falls from my hands. I watch in frustration as the paper bag sinks into a puddle and my items hit the pavement.

"Shit."

The can of whipped cream rolls across the lot as if it's on a personal mission to escape before stopping at the boots of a man with mirth in his eyes. Even without the uniform on I recognize the courier instantly. His face is not one that's easily forgotten. He bends down slowly to look at the can, and I watch every movement with bated breath. The tension of words we haven't spoken hangs heavy in the air once again, like every other interaction this week.

What are the odds I'd end up seeing the eye candy of a delivery driver on Sunday after all?

"Thank you," I say as he approaches me and holds out the can.

He offers one of those megawatt smiles I've grown accustom to seeing in the last week and winks. *Freaking winks.* I swear, he's just fucking with me. "Fun night planned?"

"I wish." My eyes widen at the words that just left my mouth. *Why the fuck did I say that?* The smile he offers me has the chill completely retreating from my body as I awkwardly laugh off the voiced thought that should have stayed internal. "I mean, no. It's for an ice cream social tomorrow."

"Ah, not my idea of a good time." A small smirk pulls at the corner of his mouth.

"What's your idea of a good time, then?" The cold must have my brain on autopilot because I can't seem to stop saying inappropriate shit. Although my question may have crossed into dangerous territory, the mischievous glint in his eyes suggests he's got a few internal thoughts of his own.

"Not ice cream in December." He laughs.

I'm standing in the parking lot with chocolate syrup, whipped cream, and sprinkles hugged to my chest, asking my delivery driver what he prefers to do with food toppings. Maybe Liv was right... "Well, I should get going." I squeeze the items tighter with my left arm and pull the car key from my pocket, managing to keep everything off the ground this time.

When the car beeps, he pulls open my door. "Let me help."

I'm a bit taken aback by his forwardness, but still slide into the driver's seat, setting down my small haul and looking back at him with a smile. That tantalizing scent pours off him with the proximity, making me feel a whole other level of warmth. Whatever he has on is an aphrodisiac in itself. And as he stands in the cold telling me to have a good rest of my evening, I make a rash decision my best friend would praise me for. He already confirmed he's single, so let's hope shooting my shot isn't an airball.

"Do you want to hang out sometime?" I blurt before I can change my mind.

He pulls his forest green stocking cap further down over his ears, and the corner of his lip slides up in a seductive show of satisfaction. "Yeah, Jules. I'd like that." His tone is almost one of relief, as if he's been waiting for me to ask.

The way he says my name may as well have me melting into the leather seat. I press the start button on my car and slide my hands beneath my thighs for warmth. "How do you feel about..." I bite my lip and pause, trying to figure out how to word what I really want to ask. He seems like a nice guy, so I'm not positive asking him to be a booty call would go over well. But I definitely don't want to give the impression that I'm looking for anything more. Ty ensured all men would be ruined for me for eternity with his bullshit.

The courier, who's name I haven't even asked for, must have taken my silence as an opportunity to guess my thoughts and answer the question I didn't finish. "I'm happy to give you my number."

"Sure." I smile softly and dig my phone out of my satchel. My fingers are finally working again as I pass it to him. "I'll just... call you sometime."

He pulls a glove off and quickly types his number in. Hitting call, his phone starts ringing in the pocket of his jeans, and he hangs up. "Have fun with your ice cream party."

With a nod, I toss my phone into the seat beside me. "You too."

He laughs and shuts my door before I can backtrack. I'm all sorts of flustered by whatever just possessed me to be so emboldened, and my brain clearly forgot that the man isn't someone I will be seeing tomorrow.

But while my heart beats hard in my chest, I realize that it's not out of fear, but excitement. And as I watch him walk through the parking lot, his jeans hugging his ass perfectly with each step, I remind myself of Liv's words.

You deserve to have fun, Jules.

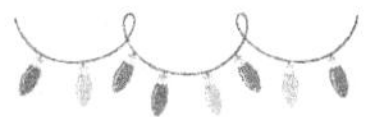

The cinnamon whiskey burns on its way down as I place the shot glass on the counter and squeeze my eyes shut. It's been a long day, and every time someone used the whipped cream at the ice cream social this afternoon, I thought of the delivery driver in the parking lot yesterday. Considering I actually had to go into the office, I wasn't home for today's daily dose of him and I mind that more than I'd like to admit.

Should I even call him on a Monday? Do I seem too desperate if I call him the day after he gave me his number?

Fuck it.

My eyes open, and I reach for my phone. I scroll to my recent calls and realize he saved his name along with his number. *Samuel, hmmm.*

I haven't drunk enough to feel buzzed, but the liquid courage from the single shot has me finally letting my guard down.

Want to come ove—

delete

So, what exactly do you do with whipped cream in Dece—

delete

Who has two thumbs and wants to get f—

DELETE

I sigh, clearly unable to play it cool on any level. Ultimately deciding to settle for something safe, I hit call. He answers almost immediately, but I stay quiet on the line for a minute, still unsure what I want to say.

"Hello?" he says again. I exhale before relaxing my shoulders and picking my chin up.

"Hey." My eyes glance at the bottle on the counter. Maybe I need to be a bit more inebriated before this turns into a twenty-question bore fest. Decidedly, I refrain from drinking anymore and channel the empowered Jules from earlier.

"What's up?" His tone is jovial, and I can hear whatever voices are in the background becoming more faint. Oh God, I called him while he was busy.

"Sorry if I interrupted something."

A deep chuckle that sends warmth directly to the pit of my belly emits through the speakers. "Saving me more like. Please tell me you have an emergency and I need to leave this dinner with my father's most annoying acquaintances."

I smile and relax a bit more at that. "I mean, I don't know if I'd call it an emergency. But there's a half-full bottle of whipped cream that didn't get used today in my fridge."

There's a long pause, and I start to think I've taken it too far. My hand grips the cool glass bottle of whiskey, and I twist the cap open. Before I can start pouring, he finally answers, "Are you saying you have no one to have dessert with?"

"That's exactly what I'm saying."

I can hear the smile in his voice this time. "A gentleman would never leave you to eat alone. Sounds like a true emergency."

He's actually willing to come over...

I take a deep, steeling breath, shakily releasing the air from my lungs and reminding myself that this can be casual. He can't cheat if it's casual. He can't fuck his secretary if it's casual. He can't lie to me about how her baby isn't his if it's casual. Anger begins to rise in my chest once again, and I shake the thought from my mind. That man in the past isn't worth my time.

"Samuel?" It's the first time I've even spoken his name, and here I am about to say the most honest thing I won't ever be able to take back.

"Yeah?"

"I don't want a gentleman."

Silence.

15 seconds...

30 seconds...

"Can you give me twenty minutes?"

My stomach flutters. "Yep."

"See you soon."

I quickly hang up and grip the counter for purchase.

Shit. This is really about to happen.

And I'm *excited* for it.

Chapter 4

Samuel

My father wasn't even at the damn dinner tonight. And I know he does this shit on purpose, urging me to take over business discussions in his place with men who I have no interest in, with no regards for the fact that I'm in the busiest season at work, and have to work in the morning. If I knew he wouldn't stop my sister's trust fund payments, I'd have told him to shove it up his ass already.

I turn my phone off as I walk up the steps to Jules' apartment. I'll receive a call from Dad soon enough asking why the hell I ended dinner so early, but that's tomorrow's problem. My knuckles rap against her front door, and in no time at all, she pulls it wide. Her blonde hair falls in loose curls over her shoulder.

The oversized T-shirt and shorts she's wearing make me feel like an asshole. I'm in a navy sports coat, ridiculously expensive dress pants, and my most polished shoes. Dressed to perfection for my dad's circus monkeys.

"Hi." I smile sheepishly, a little more self-conscious that I probably should have changed.

Those ice-blue eyes trail my body, "Oh, um… hi."

Yeah, I hate it, too.

I linger in the doorway like a damn vampire waiting for permission to cross the threshold into her home until she finally pulls the door wider and gestures inside. "Sorry for the mess. I'm still unpacking."

"No worries," I say, brushing past her and into the entryway. Immediately, I shrug out of the dumbass sports jacket and sling it over my arm.

"You can just lay that on the table over there." She points to the dining area, which is easy to see in the open-floor layout of her apartment. "Everything else has stuff on it."

"Leading me to the kitchen already, sweetheart?" A grin splits my face, and I relish in the heat that creeps up her neck.

"You *are* here for dessert," she playfully chides.

Once I've followed her instruction, I rest my ass against the edge of the table and unbutton the cuffs of my shirt. She watches as I roll them up my forearms; observing every movement, and stays firmly planted in the foyer. I look around her living space. Most of her things are still in boxes, giving me no insight into her at all, so I settle for small talk, hoping to relieve the awkward as shit, sexual tension that always seems to hang between us.

"So, what do you do for work?"

"I'm going to stop you there." Jules holds up a hand. "No occupations."

"No occupations?" My brows furrow.

"Right. I don't want to *get to know you.*"

Shit, she's setting ground rules, and I haven't even been here five minutes. There is a real fear in her eyes as she waits for me to respond; I suddenly realize that it's because if she knows me, she might get hurt. This girl is jaded.

But she's communicating her needs—I can respect that. "All right, fair enough." I click my tongue. "But you already know *my* occupation." My voice is laced with mirth in hopes of keeping the mood light.

Her full lips twist at my statement. "I do, and you also know my last name. So... we're even." She's walking toward where I'm perched with slow, purposeful strides until she's stopped mere inches in front of me.

"Forgive me for trying to be a gentleman, Jules."

"I told you." She swallows hard. "I don't want a gentleman."

"Ah, that's right." I reach out and grab her hips, pulling her so close that our lips are almost brushing. Her breath hitches as she instinctively grips my forearms. "I guess I don't have to worry about fucking you like a lady then."

A fiery lust flashes through her irises, and our mouths collide. She tastes like cinnamon and my darkest desires. Her fingers are laced tightly in my hair as she continues to explore my mouth. I groan at the pleasure-filled pain when she pulls hard, and I can already feel my cock hardening in my pants—I have no doubt she can too.

My fingers skate beneath the hem of her shirt, and I grin against her mouth at the small shiver that shoots through her. Pulling back, I speak against her lips. "Where is that whipped cream?"

Mischief causes her to smile, and I feel the cool loss of her body against mine when she walks across the kitchen and opens her fridge. She pops the lid and squirts some into her mouth; a small bit is left on the corner of her lips that I watch hungrily as she teasingly wipes it away with her finger.

Pushing away from the table, I attempt to adjust myself without making it obvious. The pressure is damn near painful. I expect her to meet me across the room again. Instead, she disappears through a door a bit further down the hall, and I'm more than eager to follow.

By the time I reach her bedroom, she's pulled the shirt from her body and dropped it right inside the door; a few more steps in, her bra is lying beside her bed. My gaze travels to where she's leaning against her headboard, sitting cross-legged on the duvet. There's a gleam in her eyes that's amplified by the low-lit lamp on her side table. The sight makes me groan.

Casual and I have never been a thing, and I may have over-committed to this siren when I promised to keep it that way.

"I'm never going to look at dessert the same again." I grin, unbuttoning my shirt as I walk toward her. It falls to the floor, and she giggles.

"Is this the part where I tell you to crawl to me?"

"I'm not sure your bed is quite big enough for that, but I'll happily get on my knees for you, sweetheart."

Her smile doesn't falter, but the reaction from her body is saccharine sweet as those blue eyes stay firmly on me. My hands move to the button of my pants, and I slide them down my legs, leaving them pooled on the carpet. I bend down to peel my socks off next, and she shakes her head. "Socks stay on."

I pause and raise an inquisitive eyebrow.

"If you take your socks off, it's not as casual."

Barking a laugh, I concede and move to the hem of my boxers, "Am I allowed to discard these? Sorry, I forgot to read the handbook," I joke and offer her a playful wink.

"Yes... as a matter of fact"—she shifts to her knees, that beautiful body on full display for me— "I'll help."

I'm not sure what I expected, but her retrieving the whipped cream and getting on all fours was not on my bingo card.

Fucking hell.

I watch with a carnal desire as *she's* the one crawling to *me*. How she manages to look sexy with the can in her hand is a fucking conundrum. "You know, Samuel." The devil in her flashes in those pretty little eyes. "I want to test a theory."

She stops in front of me, rising onto her knees. Even with the bed beneath her, she still doesn't match my height, and I look down. "Oh yeah, what's that?"

A smirk pulls at the corner of her mouth. "*Everything* is better whipped."

"Is that so?" I query, playing into her game. My eyes fall to where she's popped the top of the can.

"Yep." She begins shaking the topping before placing it beside her. "There's only one issue." Blue-painted fingers hook into the hem of my underwear, and she finally frees my painfully hard cock from its confines. "That's better."

I catch her chin beneath my fingers and bring her face to look at me. "Lay down."

She's been in control the whole time we've been in this room, and while I'll respect her ground rules, relinquishing control isn't something I've ever been good at.

Shaking her head, she shocks me when she simply says, "No."

I capture her lips in mine, and as I feel her begin to melt into me, I give a hard slap to her ass cheek, causing a scream to reverberate between us. When she pulls back, a hint of surprise and lust blend into her features. "I'm sorry, I thought you said everything was better whipped," I jest.

"Seems my theory was correct." She breathes a laugh and kisses me again. I smile against her mouth and snake my hands behind her thighs, pulling hard until she's on her back. "That's not fair," she cries.

"I don't play around with my food, Jules." With that, I hook my pointer fingers in the sides of her underwear and tear them away. Once every perfect inch of her is on display, I drop to my knees and lift her legs over my shoulders.

"Well, in that case..." She picks up the can of whipped topping and sprays a good amount on each of her peaked nipples.

As I lick up her center, I wasn't expecting to need her as badly as I do, but one taste leaves me unable to tear myself away. She moans and snakes her hands into my hair, pulling hard with each cry of pleasure that spills from her throat. Finally, I remove my tongue and replace it with two fingers, continuing to pump in and out of her while my mouth teases every inch of her glorious body until I'm cleaning the food from her breasts.

"Please," she begs. "I need more."

Without a word, I insert a third finger and suck a pert nipple into my mouth, flicking my tongue over the peak while picking up the pace of my fingers inside of her. Her back begins arching from the bed. I can sense her impending orgasm and bite into her thigh, sending her over the edge in pleasure as she screams, "Samuel!"

"Careful, sweetheart. Your neighbors might find out who you're getting casual with."

A breathless laugh leaves her as she closes her eyes and rolls her head back onto the mattress. "You're a fucking menace."

"And I'm not even done yet," I say, standing with a dark grin on my face.

She opens her eyes and runs her tongue along her lips, shuffling to wrap her legs around my waist as I line myself up with her entrance and slowly push in. We both groan in pleasure as I fill her completely. If her taste wasn't enough to do me in, the feeling of being inside her has me throwing caution to the wind.

No way in fuck am I going to be able to be casual with Jules Harrington, but I'll try as long as she'll let me.

Chapter 5

Jules

"Yes, Kimberly. My love life is great. I tried to have a one-night-stand with my delivery driver and now we've been sleeping together for weeks," I admit sarcastically to myself. Shaking my head at the thought of saying that to my mom. "Fuck, Jules. No. You can't tell her that." I groan, placing the palms of my hands to my forehead.

Great, now I'm talking to myself too.

There's no amount of shower rehearsal that can prepare me for my exasperating mother. I should have just told her I wasn't feeling well, but after moving to an entirely new country, the thought of not seeing my parents for Christmas is depressing.

I rinse the rest of the shampoo from my hair and stand beneath the torrent of water for a bit longer. Closing my eyes, I roll my shoulders back. Centering myself in this moment of peace before enduring the next few days.

"A one-night-stand, huh?" I'm so lost in thought that Samuel's voice is a jump scare. The next thing I know, my ass is hitting the slick tiled floor of the shower.

"SHIT!"

"Fuck, Jules, are you okay?" Samuel flings the door open, and I throw my hands across my chest to cover myself.

"You know I've seen it all, right?" There's a mischievous gleam in those deep brown irises as he turns off the shower and offers me his hand.

"I'm aware," I snap. "But staying overnight is one thing, seeing me naked in the shower the next morning is another."

"Careful, sweetheart. Next thing you know, we'll be *dating*." He says the last word with humor, yet it still elicits a full-body shudder from me.

"Yeah, no." I take his outstretched hand and allow him to help me up. The urge to rub my sore ass is strong, but my arm stays firmly planted across my chest.

"What are you even doing in here?" Snatching a towel from the hook, I wrap it around myself and await his answer.

"Well, since you only have one bathroom and I have to go to work soon, I thought I might brush my teeth." He lifts his hand and it's only then that I notice he's holding a toothbrush.

My eyes widen. "You did *not* bring your own toothbrush to my apartment?" I'm horrified. First, it's the toothbrush; next, it's a duffle; then, a full-blown closet full of gray sweatpants and old tees. *Though, the gray sweatpants I wouldn't mind...*

"Jules, you texted me at one in the morning on a Thursday. It was a fair assumption that I wouldn't be going home afterward." He shrugs and turns back to finish his task. This beautiful man is damn near naked in front of me, his black hair disheveled in a just-fucked way, with only a pair of boxers covering his essentials, and all I can focus on is one thing.

"So, you brought an... *overnight bag?*" *Did I just manifest this shit?* The words make my stomach drop. Ty was the last man who stayed overnight in my bed, and he broke my heart so thoroughly that I swore off men altogether. I made good on that promise for a whole year before last night. Somehow, Samuel has managed to break down the wall I've spent the last year building, and the thought of that made me nervous.

Shit.

Samuel shrugs and meets my gaze in the mirror. He offers me a wink as he finishes brushing his teeth and retrieves his beard oil from a small toiletry bag. The muscles of his back flex as he works, keeping my eyes glued to him. How in the hell he manages to make basic hygiene sexy is beyond me. I shake my head to clear it. *This is just a hookup.*

I'm not sure why I texted him last night. He's right; it was way too late for recreational sex. I have to get that damned wall back in check.

Mentally grabbing my bricks and mortar, I stand straighter and assert my stipulations. "Okay, new rule. No late-night sex on weekdays."

"You got it," Samuel agrees easily as he smiles and gestures to the shower behind me. "Do you mind?"

"What?"

"If I shower?"

"Oh, of course not. Go ahead." I step out of the way, still reeling from the whole interaction. No one is this cheerful at seven in the morning, especially after only four and a half hours of sleep. Spending half the night buried inside me must still have him on a dopamine high.

Not that his early morning mood should surprise me. He's sunshine embodied. Every time I'm with him, he has a smile on his face alongside the most ridiculously playful banter. He's a man who exudes golden retriever energy. Not to mention the fact that he's phenomenal in the bedroom... *and the living room and his truck and—Stop.*

I mentally pull the brakes and wrench that train right off the tracks. Samuel has been consuming far too many of my thoughts lately.

Stalking back to the bedroom, I quickly dress in a pair of leggings and a sweater, even though I know my mother will insist that I change when I see her. For the last five years of my life, I've had to wear heels and power suits every day for work. I'll be damned if I'm wearing stilettos and pencil skirts while enjoying my holiday.

At the sound of a zipper behind me, I turn to find Samuel butt-ass naked, rummaging through the contents of his bag on my bed. Memories of last night come flooding back. The way his hands left no inch of me untouched, the flex in his arms as his huge frame pressed into my body, and the feeling of every chiseled muscle beneath my palms. My thighs clench at the thought, reminding me exactly why I woke up next to this man. He's addicting.

"Dammit, Samuel. Did you not have a towel?" I roll my eyes and look away from him, feigning annoyance.

"I'm sorry, Jules. If I remember right, I had at least three parts of my body inside of you last night; surely you can stand to look at my cock for five seconds. I'm putting on my boxers, you're the one that made it a show." He flashes a wide grin, and I can't even argue.

Who can blame me?

Five minutes later, he's dressed in three layers of clothing, another reminder that the weather here in Canada isn't going to be any better than growing up in northeast Oregon. I'm not sure where Samuel is from. But, based on the very little information I have on him, he isn't a Canadian native. If it hadn't been for Liv questioning the local barista after seeing Samuel the day she came to visit, I wouldn't even know that much. I don't pry too much into his personal life. Where someone grew up seems like information people don't share when they're just fucking.

"I'm headed out. Text me later?" Samuel throws his duffle over his shoulder and stalks toward me. I take a step backward until my back hits the wall, and my chest races out of fear that he is about to kiss me goodbye. He leans in, the earthy scent of his beard oil igniting my senses as the smooth fabric of his coat brushes along my neck and over my shoulder.

A knot forms in my stomach when he brings his hand up to caress my cheek, "Don't worry, sweetheart. I'd prefer to kiss you elsewhere." With that, he turns and leaves my room.

My heart is still pounding as I slump my shoulders and release a shaky breath. A feeble attempt to get myself together. I hear the front door open, followed by a familiar deep voice that resounds from the foyer.

Dad?

Chapter 6

Samuel

I pull open the door of Jules' apartment to leave, finding an older gentleman, eyes wide, with his hand poised to either knock on her door or deck me in the face. Directly behind him is a woman, equal in age, beaming at me—a stark contrast to the less-than-thrilled expression of the man before me.

"Who the hell are you?"

Before I can answer, the petite woman behind him chimes in, "Oh my goodness, I am so sorry, it seems we have the wrong apartment?"

"Mom? Dad?"

Did she just say Mom and Dad?

I glance over my shoulder to find Jules has the same horror in her eyes as me. *Fuck, damage control.*

"Good morning, sir. Just here for a delivery."

His eyebrow raises in question. "That requires you being in my daughter's apartment?"

"It was a massive package, Dad," Jules hurries to explain. "I wasn't able to carry it in by myself."

Ha. Good save.

The amount of self-control I exhibit by not laughing at that should earn me a gold star. She's not exactly lying; I did deliver quite the package.

Her dad looks from me to his daughter. "Uh-huh."

"Hello, I'm Kimberly." Jules' mom beams at me and offers her hand. She's got the exact same blonde hair, and ice-blue eyes as her daughter.

"Good lord, Mom. You don't have to introduce yourself to my delivery driver," Jules huffs.

"Good morning, Kimberly. Samuel." I shake her hand and feel the eye roll Jules offers us without even having to turn around.

"Where is your truck?" Her dad isn't giving up the interrogation, despite his wife's warmth.

Thinking quickly on my feet, I offer a broad smile and explain. "Personal vehicle driver, sir. PVDs are quite common this time of year. 'Tis the peak season." That's not exactly true with my courier company. He doesn't need to know that, though.

He lifts his chin, arms still crossed over his chest, eyeing me with suspicion before spotting my overnight bag. His eyes narrow, and his jaw tics as if he's cracked the case. He opens his mouth to speak, but before he can get a word out, Jules' mom cuts him off.

"Charles, let the poor boy through the door. He's clearly a busy man, and it's cold as sin out here." Kimberly shivers, and Charles reluctantly follows her command, stepping aside.

"Have a good day, dear," Kimberly says, her eyes traveling all the way from my head to my toes. *Did she just body-check me?*

My thoughts are confirmed as Kimberly's voice carries through the door right before it shuts. "Oh my God, Jules. He's hot."

In unison, shouts of "Jesus, Kimberly!" and "Mom!" are the last things I hear as I rush back to my truck—which is, in fact, *not* a personal use vehicle. I laugh and shake my head at the entire interaction before getting in and blasting the heat.

While I wait for the vehicle to warm up, I pull my phone from my pocket. I *never* text Jules first. I learned quickly that it's not her style. But, right now, the opportunity is just too good to pass up.

I chuckle at her response, and head to work. That woman has me in a chokehold. She's made it exceedingly clear that she is only using me for sex. Still, there is something about her that pulls me in. Even at one in the morning on a work night, I can't say no. And I have no regrets about the exhaustion I'll be feeling today.

The mere notion of her has me smiling as I pull into my usual parking spot, step out of my truck and begin my trek to the building.

"What's got you grinning so much, bud?" I look over my shoulder and find Trent Sanderson, my neighbor and coworker, rushing to catch up with me. I quickly school my expression, wiping the stupid grin off my face, and walk faster. For being in his early sixties and a full foot shorter than me, I'm surprised when he matches me stride for stride.

"I didn't think you were seeing anyone, Donner?" Trent continues, giving me a smirk that suggests he's in on some secret.

"I'm not." I pick up my pace, hoping he will take a hint. I'm generally an outgoing guy; I'll talk to anyone about anything. Except Trent. If I let him find out an inkling of my personal life, everyone and their mother would know within an hour. Jules moved to town a month ago. I'm not about to tarnish our situationship with rumors.

"Mindy said that you left in the middle of the night and never came back," he huffs, practically jogging beside me now.

Ah, yes. *Mindy.* His nosey wife likes to keep tabs on me for whatever reason. It's creepy as hell.

"I was getting milk."

"Who the hell gets milk in the middle of the night? Come o—"

"Someone who wakes up and wants a bowl of damn Cheerios. I'll see you later, Trent." I move past him and swipe my keycard to enter the building, rushing through security and thankfully avoiding any further inquisitions.

Chapter 7

Jules

"You guys are here early."

"Sweetie, I told you our flight got in at five." My mother moves to give me a quick hug and a peck on the cheek before stepping back to look around my apartment.

"I swore you said nine. I wasn't expecting you until closer to eleven." The airport is over an hour and a half from my apartment. I thought I would have plenty of time to prepare for them.

"Oh, *we know*." She offers me a broad, knowing smile. Simultaneously, Dad and I both roll our eyes at her insinuation, and he steps forward to embrace me as well.

"So." She glances around the room, no doubt looking for the mystery package. "What did you order?"

"A treadmill," I blurt out before I can think of a better lie. I'm stuck in it now though. "I can't exactly go running outside right now with the weather, and gym memberships are expensive here." Although now that I'm thinking about it, I probably should purchase one of those. The only exercise I've gotten since moving to Coals Lake is late-night "cardio" with Samuel.

"I still can't believe you moved all the way to Canada just to work from home."

I resist yet another eye roll at her dramatic statement. "I only work from home two days out of the week, Mother."

"How are you supposed to meet anyone if you're cooped up in here? And the drive to your office… even if you *do* meet someone…it's just so far."

There it is. She gave me a month after I broke up with Ty before she started in on my dating life and hasn't let up since.

I open my mouth to explain that my promotion at Donner Logging Company puts me in charge of all marketing operations for their Canadian offices. The Calgary division is where the CEO stays. I'm required to meet with him twice a week. I was also given an entire team to oversee in Lethbridge. Since I will be splitting my time between there and headquarters, Coals Lake made the most sense.

Dad speaks first, saving me from reiterating that information. "It's a smart financial decision on her part, Kimberly."

He is one of the top financial advisers at his company, giving him the professional knowledge to back me up here. With my mother being a real estate agent, she should have also understood why I chose to live in a small town outside of Calgary. Aside from the commute, my money goes further here, and I am far more comfortable in a town of ten thousand versus 1.3 million.

"Have you eaten, Jules?" Dad asks, promptly changing the subject.

"Not yet."

"Let's do that, and then we'll head back to the lodge. Those seats on the flight were impossible to sleep in." He rubs the back of his neck to further his point.

I nod in agreement and move to grab my coat.

"Are you going to change, dear?" My mother's eyes roam over my casual attire.

I didn't even have time to throw my hair into a bun when they arrived, far too concerned with racing to the door when Samuel opened it for them. I'm surprised she waited this long to say something. "Nope. I'm on holiday."

Her lips press into a taut line, and I ignore the contempt in her expression as Dad ushers us out the door.

The rest of the morning is spent with my mother rapid-firing questions about my love life. By the afternoon, there have been at least ten mentions of Samuel. I continuously explain that I don't know him outside of the occasional delivery. She tsks and tells me *she'd* be ordering packages daily if he were her driver. Consequently, earning her an annoyed grumble from my father.

Four hours later, I'm finally sinking onto my couch. My feet are sore, and the coffee has definitely worn off. After we finished at the cafe, my mother insisted we walk around the town center. While the festive Christmas decorations were beautiful, she was clearly the only one who got enough sleep last night as Dad and I trudged along behind her. I close my eyes, nearly succumbing to the exhaustion, when my phone rings. As much as I want to ignore it, when I see Olivia's name on the screen, I ultimately answer.

"How's Delivery Daddy?" She wastes no time in bringing up Samuel.

"For the love, Liv, please quit calling him that."

"Oh, come on. We can't all be God's favorite. I need to live vicariously through you," she pouts. She ended whatever she was with Audrey a couple of weeks ago, so I know she's keeping tabs on Samuel and me as a distraction.

"We're sleeping together; that hardly makes me God's favorite... I don't even know his full name." *Shit, that sounds bad.*

"Uh huh... Well, if you don't want him, I'd be happy to take your place."

I laugh out loud. "You don't even like men."

"That's not true. I'm heteroflexible. Besides, I like that one guy."

"My brother?" I cringe at the memory of the day I found out they slept together. He's twelve years older than us.

"Yeah, him. Too bad he's married."

Yeah, we're getting off this subject ASAP. "What are you doing for Christmas?"

"Same thing I do every year, Jules. Getting wine drunk and disappointing my family. Don't change the subject."

I find my reprieve from continuing this conversation in the form of an incoming call. A local number I don't recognize lights up the screen and I'm thankful for the distraction. "Hey, Liv, I've got another call coming in. I've gotta let you go. Love you." I hang up to the sound of her protests and answer the call.

"Hello?"

"Hey, Jules. It's Mary. I'm sorry to call you while we are on holiday. I just wanted to let you know that I received an email from Mr. Donner informing me that you will be introduced at the company Christmas party on Sunday." *What?* "I'm in charge of the planning and didn't want you to be blindsided."

"Oh, wow. Okay. Thank you for letting me know, Mary." I rake a hand through my hair in exasperation. A formal introduction at the party is the last thing I want, but I can't exactly tell Mary no if it was Mr. Donner's idea.

"Of course, we are very excited to have you on the team. While I'm finalizing everything, will you be bringing a guest?"

For some ridiculous reason, my mind veers to Samuel. No way in hell would I be bringing my late-night booty call to a black-tie Christmas party.

"No, just me."

"Sounds good. We will see you Sunday!" she says cheerfully, and I thank her again before disconnecting the call.

I need a freaking nap after the mental overload of this day.

Before I close my eyes, I pull up my text conversation with Samuel and do something I know I shouldn't.

That will be tomorrow's problem.

Chapter 8

Samuel

Come over tonight.

I grin and slip my phone back into my pocket. "I've got this one; it needs a signature. If you want to start looking for the next stop, that would be great. It should be on the top shelf in the back."

Paul nods and heads to the back of the truck while I haul the giant wine box. He could have gotten the signature, but he struggles with any package over fifty pounds. Unfortunately for me, that's half of my truck today. Everyone seems to be getting their last-minute wine deliveries before the holiday, and to my dismay, getting signatures hasn't been nearly as exciting as the day I knocked on Jules' door.

I stop the thoughts before they take over. I'll get plenty of her tonight.

Silently, I thank Mr. and Mrs. Landry for shoveling their walkway and adding a generous amount of salt. So many haven't after the storm on Tuesday, and it's been a bitch to haul shit to everyone's porches through inches of fresh powder. I ring the doorbell and take a step back. Within a minute, the front door is pulled open.

"Hey, Mr. Landry. I've got some wine that needs a signature." I pass him the box and pull up the screen I need him to sign.

He scribbles his name and hands the device back to me. "Thanks, Samuel. Working hard today?"

"I'm definitely staying busy," I reply with a shrug.

"'Tis the season," he chuckles. "You stay warm."

"Oh, I'll try," I quip with a smile, even though I mentally curse every single person who says that to me. How the hell am I supposed to stay warm when it's ten-below out here?

The next five hours seem to drag as I find myself anticipating the night, but I'm finally finished for the day. Getting into my truck, I retrieve my phone from my pocket to text Jules back. One thing I fucking love about her is that she doesn't care whether I respond in two minutes or five business days. She never double-texts.

As my thumbs move to respond, a phone call from my dad pops up, and I accidentally answer.

"Hello, son." His voice resounds through the cab.

Dammit. "Hey, Dad. What's up?"

"I'm calling to confirm you'll be at the Christmas party this weekend."

I internally groan. The last thing I want to do is dress up in a pretentious suit and save face with the pompous assholes my father works with. "I've already told you, Dad, I'll probably have to work. It's a busy time of year."

"You don't work on Sundays." His tone is clipped.

"How about I promise to make the next one?" I respond in jest.

"No, Samuel. That is not an option. You will be there." Again, he leaves no room for rebuttal.

Alexander Donner is one of the most successful CEOs in the country. He's built a name for himself in the logging industry. If there is one thing I can say about my father, it's that he is a powerhouse of a man. Not someone who takes no for an answer... or appreciates when you leave a business dinner early.

"Fine," I concede. "Is Morgan going to be there?"

"Yes, and I would love for my son to be there as well. You're going to run this company someday. You're thirty with a master's degree slinging packages around." *Yes, because my job is so easy, Father.* "If you're not working for me within the next year, I am pulling your trust."

"I don't need it. That isn't exactly a threat."

"It is when Morgan is involved. I will see you Sunday, Samuel." The phone disconnects, leaving me with nothing but the sound of a purring engine.

I sit in the parking lot for a moment longer. My thoughts warring between the excitement I had felt about seeing Jules tonight, and resenting my father for refusing to accept the life I've made for myself.

The idea of his only son working a blue-collar job when I could be sitting in a cozy office pulling funds from my trust is preposterous to him.

My father has been asking me for years to run his company, and I refuse every time he revisits the conversation. I grew up watching the way he ran Donner Logging Company. He was never home. Too invested in his work to form any sort of paternal bond with his children. Not to say I didn't have a privileged life. I'm very thankful. But after working with him for three months when I graduated from college, I quickly realized that I didn't want my future to look like my childhood.

As my anger rises, I turn my attention back to Jules, focusing on humor to cut through the contempt for my father.

I read her text again. The fact that she doesn't ask, only demands, probably says a lot about me, considering I'll one-hundred-and-ten percent be knocking on her door in the next hour. Still, I can't help but fuck with her.

> I just got off work. Want to go get dinner first?

> Ew. No. Eat before you come.

> I always do.

Chapter 9

Jules

The minute I open the door, Samuel picks me up and my legs wrap around his waist. My back slams hard enough against the wall to leave me breathless. He kicks the door closed behind him, and in an instant, his mouth is on mine. With one hand cupping my ass, he allows the wall to take the bulk of my weight as he grips my hair, yanking my head back. I suck in a breath, the force bringing tears to my eyes as a fire blazes in my core.

For someone as sweet as Samuel, he's never gentle with me, a desire I didn't realize I had until three weeks ago when we first began this little situationship. He's truly allowed me to explore my sexual preferences. From the moment we met, there's been a physical respect and understanding between us, reassuring me that despite his jokes this morning, he still treats whatever we have as it is: pure sex. No strings attached.

Wasting no time, he kicks off his shoes before I'm pulling his shirt up his abdomen and over his head. I haphazardly toss it to the ground, and he follows the gesture, removing my own shirt with the same furious need. His dark eyes dilate as he realizes I'm bare beneath the fabric. I bring my hands up to brush through his hair. Only then do I notice it's wet. He must have gone home long enough to shower before coming over. The scent of that damn body wash ignites me like the aphrodisiac it is.

I catch a glimpse of his flexed back muscles in the mirror above the entryway table as he removes his hand from my hair to caress my breasts while kissing my neck. The scratch marks I left on his shoulders last night are still prominent. My nails threaten to make new ones at the sensation of his fingers teasing my nipples.

"Fuck, Jules." The first words either of us have spoken since he arrived.

"I need you," I whimper as he moves the lace of my underwear to the side.

There's no teasing, only instant fullness as he gives me exactly what I want and slips two fingers in. A mischievous grin splits his face at finding me so ready for him, and he leans in to whisper in my ear. "Look at yourself, sweetheart, whimpering and wet for me. Watch me make you fall apart." He nips at my ear, and I shudder at the sensation of it all. Obeying him and meeting my own gaze in the mirror, I'm rewarded with his thumb on my clit. He begins pumping his hand into me, and I'm captivated by every movement.

He picks up the pace, fucking me so thoroughly with only his fingers that I already feel my walls tightening around him. Moving his head down to suck one of my nipples into his mouth, he follows the flick of his tongue with a sharp bite, and I cry out. "Samuel!"

I'm on the brink of orgasm when he leans in and growls, "As pretty as you look pinned against this wall screaming my name, I'd rather fuck you on every surface of this apartment."

I groan at the loss as our mouths clash once again. A moment later, he removes his fingers, and I feel every bit of that loss. He carries me from the foyer to my dining room table. When my ass hits the edge of the wood, I firmly place my hands beneath me, stopping the descent and effectively causing him to pause. "Samuel, you cannot fuck me on this table. My parents are going to eat here tomorrow."

"And I'll be eating here tonight." Strong hands trail from my waist to my thighs, gripping hard and making me yelp. "Besides, I believe I was instructed to eat before I come." I smirk at the joke before he's pulling me hard enough by his grip on my thighs that my back hits the table. A groan releases from him as he fully removes my panties. In the next breath, his mouth is on my pussy.

Samuel is one of those men that women refer to as having a "magic tongue." Not only is he a fucking magician with his mouth, but he's a pleaser. *Shit. He really is the whole package.* His tongue flicks along my clit, bringing me back to the now. My eyelids flutter closed, and his name spills from my lips again.

"Eyes on me." I look up to find his gaze dark, and hooded with desire, locking with mine. This man is sin. Pure sin. Though, I can't find it in me to repent. "I'm going to taste every last drop of you as you come, and then I'm going to fuck you until you can't walk tomorrow."

My chest heaves as I watch his head lower back down between my legs. His tongue thrusts into me, and anticipation adds to the overall sensation he's providing. I work my fingers in deliberate movements over my clit, unable to keep my hands from roaming. He swats them away. "That's my job, sweetheart." He doesn't look up as he reprimands me, taking over with his own hand. I don't have the ability to keep myself still, so I settle on gripping his hair and urging him on.

Just as I'm about to finish, he moves his tongue to my clit and inserts his fingers once again, curling them inside of me. My nerve endings are on fire, his mouth moving with such fervor while his fingers hit that sweet spot inside of me. It's all too much. My back arches off the table and I come hard.

A dark chuckle leaves his mouth, working me through my orgasm before inspecting his fingers. The evidence of my arousal is more than prominent. "I don't think you're wet enough." His features swim with humor at the sarcastic comment. I know he's joking because I'm fucking soaked.

I don't have time to comprehend, let alone respond, before I'm whisked up once again and find myself in his arms, being carried toward the couch. Just as he is about to place me on the cushions, I twist in his arms, and my feet hit the ground. He's so caught off guard by the sudden movement that he falls back onto the recliner behind him with the simple push of his shoulders. What I intend to be a sexy show of power, results in the back of the recliner snapping when all of Samuel's body weight falls against it. Still gripping my hand, I let out a surprised gasp as he pulls me over with him. The next thing I know, his erection is pressing through his sweats, making itself known against my thigh while my tits are suffocating his face and he's laughing beneath me.

"I think if I had to pick one way to go, this would be it." His muffled voice meets my ears, and I can't help but match his boyish grin. Pushing myself up and giving the man some space to breathe, our eyes lock, and for the first time in a long time, I feel an attraction to a man beyond physical.

Fuck.

Before I can allow my brain to have any further reaction, he moves us, so that he's flat on his back on the floor and I'm straddling him. His eyes light up as if a thought just occurred to him. Without warning, he slips his arms to the inside of my thighs and lifts me, sliding my body down his forearms and directly onto his face. Any prior hesitation I had is lost as his tongue once again finds my center. My hips instinctively grind against his mouth, his beard creating a euphoric friction, and my hands find the wall in front of me. Within minutes, I'm coming all over again, and I can feel the smile spread across his lips without even opening my eyes.

"You know, I lied." He rolls us over and stands before continuing, "*That* would be my ideal way to go."

I shake my head with a breathless laugh, and Samuel offers his hand to help me up. But he will do no such thing. Instead, I sit on my knees, grip the waistband of his sweats, and with one sharp tug, they're pooled on the floor at his feet. I look up at him through my lashes as my tongue traces a path from the base of his cock all the way to the tip.

A breathy "fuck" leaves his lips as his hands tangle in my hair, guiding my mouth down his full length. I gag as he hits the back of my throat. The low hum of ecstasy he gives in return urges me on. My fingernails grip his ass as he uses his hold on my hair to thrust his cock into my mouth. His pace quickens. He's attempting to take over.

I lean back, locking eyes with him. The usual gleam of sunshine is now replaced with a fiery lust. "Let me." His jaw tics. Samuel doesn't easily relinquish control when it comes to pleasure, but I don't care. I grip the base of his cock and slide my hand up and down his shaft a few times before wetting my mouth and sliding the length of him past my lips. My tongue works in slow, deliberate movements, twirling from the tip of his dick down to the base and back up again as I tighten my mouth around him.

Finally, I squeeze the back of his thigh and push him all the way to the back of my throat

signaling to him that he can take the reins.

"Hold on, sweetheart." The way his lips curve slightly at the corners has me bracing myself on his thighs just before the tip of his cock assaults my throat. The repeated motion as he fucks my mouth has tears trailing my cheeks.

Abruptly, Samuel pulls out of my mouth and grips my chin, pulling me to stand, and without any words, he crushes his lips to mine.

Our tongues clash in a frenzied kiss as he steps out of his pants and walks me backward. I don't even care where he is taking me; every fiber of my being is begging for his cock. Samuel is nothing if not thorough, and I know the wait will be worth it. My back hits the bookcase of my entertainment center. He grips himself and slides the tip of his erection up my center, feeling exactly how much I need him right now.

"You want me inside you, sweetheart?" I whimper at his words while my core throbs with need. He trails kisses and small nips down my neck to my chest, then sucks my nipple into his mouth as his fingers torment my clit. "Say it."

"Oh, for fuck's sake, Samuel, fuck me already."

He releases a dark chuckle, and the world spins as I'm flipped around to face the entertainment center. In quick succession, Samuel pushes his thick cock inside me, and my head lolls back against his shoulder as he slows his movements to allow my body to adjust to his size.

I moan, pushing my ass back and forcing him deeper inside of me. With one last slow thrust, he grips my throat and pulls out of me. "Good girl. Now, let the neighbors hear how well you take every inch of me." This is the only warning I receive before he's slamming into me. Doing exactly what I demanded and fucking me relentlessly. I cry out, unintentionally giving him what he wanted in return. I can't be bothered to worry about who will hear us right now, though.

I scramble to grip the entertainment center. Thuds resound around the room as my books fall off the shelves with how forcefully he's thrusting into me.

Glass shattering threatens to pull me out of focus, but the grip Samuel has on my throat tightens, and I don't give my broken possessions a second thought.

My orgasm builds as his thrusts become dangerously close to sending me over the edge. His free hand grips my breast, his fingers finding my nipple while he simultaneously bites into my shoulder. The pain mixed with pleasure is enough to make me see stars, and the force of my orgasm has me crying out curses. I feel him follow me into the abyss at the telling jerk of his cock inside me.

Our chests heave, both of us fighting to catch our breaths. He places a soft kiss on the top of my head and pulls me back into his arms. I don't allow myself to think about the fact that I allow him to, let alone that I enjoy it.

Chapter 10

Samuel

Jules melts into me, and I can't deny that she fits perfectly against my chest. Our breaths fall in sync. Both of us coming down from the high. This doesn't feel like friends with benefits anymore. The connection I feel to her is stronger than that, not that I could ever speak that out loud. It would just cause her to have a panic attack at the thought of this situationship being any more than what she says it is.

Finding a distraction to remove those thoughts, I view her living room, which is now in shambles. The recliner is broken in half, and there are at least ten books lying in a puddle of water alongside poinsettias from a broken vase. *Shit.*

Reluctantly, I release her and step carefully around the broken glass. Bending down to pick up one of the novels, I sigh. "I'm sorry. I'll get you new ones."

Her eyes track my movements and widen. "Dammit. That's a signed copy." The statement makes me feel bad as I collect the rest of the fallen books. They're sopping wet and unsalvageable.

"Jesus, Jules. How many male torsos did I destroy?" I swear, with each title I see, the males become less clothed. I flip another cover to further my point.

She laughs, and the sound lights me up, causing an involuntary grin to spread across my face. "Technically, that's his back, not his torso," she retorts as she retrieves her ruined literature. "And look, both of these guys are clothed!"

"Okay, fair. Make me a list and I will replace your paper porn."

"Paper porn?"

"That man looks like he is rolling up his sleeves to screw someone seven ways to Sunday," I say, taking the novel that's currently sitting on the top of her pile and opening to a random page. They're all stuck together from the water, but I laugh as my point is proven. "Jules, this says '*cock*' four times on one page."

She rolls her eyes and snatches the book from me. "You don't have to replace anything, Samuel. I don't want you to. I've read all of them. These are only trophies for my bookshelf. I'll order new ones on Tuesday. You guys have enough to deliver at the moment."

I don't give a shit about increasing my volume. It's just another excuse to see her anyway. I'll be ordering new ones for her tonight. I choose to save the argument and point to the recliner, "And that?"

"Sir. We are both naked, standing in my living room, you just tainted the table my parents will be eating Christmas dinner on, and an eighth of my books are ruined. I do not have the mental capacity to worry about my broken recliner."

The remaining stack of soaked books is still in my hand, so I simply chuckle at the table comment and change the subject. "Do you want me to throw these away?"

The most dramatic gasp I've ever heard releases from her and a hand flies to cover her mouth. She's looking at me as if I've just admitted I'm some sort of serial killer.

"You never throw away books. They can be repurposed. What the hell?"

"Umm…okay?" My brow furrows in confusion. *What is she possibly going to do with these?*

"I'll grab a towel. You can set them on the kitchen counter." I shake my head at this exasperating woman and watch her bare ass sway as she retreats without another word.

"Here," She returns and spreads the towel on the counter. Following her instruction, I set the stack of books on it. To my utter dismay, she threw on a T-shirt while she was gone and retrieved my clothing.

"I should probably head out," I say as I dress. I'm fucking starving but know that if I offer her dinner again, she may physically fight me. "How long are your parents in town?"

"Until Sunday."

"They aren't staying for Christmas?" I raise an eyebrow. It seems odd that they would travel all the way to Coals Lake and not celebrate the holiday with her.

"No, my brother and his wife are flying to Portland this year so they're celebrating with me now and him the morning of."

I glance at the kitchen table. "Well, I hope they enjoy their meal. I know I did." I wink, and her cheeks flush.

"Why don't you go eat actual dinner? I've got paper porn to read," she teases.

"Do you want me to at least move your recliner?"

"Girl power, Samuel. I'll get it."

I run a hand down my face. If there is one thing I've learned about Jules these last three weeks, it's that she is one of the most independent and stubborn women I've ever met. "I know you can do it yourself, but I'm half responsible for breaking it."

"I said I've got it." She waves me off, clearly getting irritated.

"Okay, if you're sure." I head to the foyer and slip on my shoes. "I'll see ya later, sweetheart." She offers me a brief smile and wastes no time shutting the door as soon as I cross the threshold.

I feel like an asshole for leaving her to clean up the mess, so I sit in the parking lot and order new books for her while the titles are still fresh in my mind. If she won't let me carry the chair, this is the least I can do.

Twenty minutes later, I'm pulling into my drive when Mindy trudges through the snow toward me. *It's 11:30 at night, why the fuck is she outside?*

Hoping to avoid whatever inquisitions she has prepared, I pull into the garage and pretend I don't see her. I'm a fool to think that would be any use, though. She pops her head around the corner just as I slam my truck door closed.

"What are you doing out so late, Samuel?" Her dark hair is pinned up in tight rollers, and she's wearing a green bathrobe that is in no way fit for the harsh Canadian climate.

"I could ask the same of you," I deadpan.

"Oh, I was letting Echo out when I saw you pull in." At the mention of their Siberian husky, Echo runs into the garage to greet me. While her owners may be some of the most exasperating people on the planet, I fucking love this dog. "Surely you aren't getting home from work this late; Trent was home hours ago."

"Had some things to take care of, Mindy." I keep my answers clipped, hoping to avoid a full interrogation.

"Uh-huh, well, I hope you enjoyed your milk." She gives me an over-exaggerated wink as if she is part of some inside joke and calls Echo back to her. "See you later, Sam."

I bite my tongue at that. Despite the amount of times I've asked her not to call me Sam, she still insists on the shortened nickname. She and Trent could both benefit from learning about boundaries.

I enter my home with a sigh of relief, thankful to finally be one step closer to the end of our busiest season. Regardless of the exhaustion that comes from a physically demanding job, every day I'm delivering packages beats the three months I was forced to parade around in custom-tailored Armani suits, following orders from my father. I take satisfaction in the fact that my choice of occupation still drives him insane.

Since it's close to midnight, I decide to multitask and eat while I shop for reading chairs with two-day shipping availability for. If my father is so insistent that he will pull my sister's trust funds too if I don't use the money, then I may as well spend it on Jules.

Chapter 11

Jules

"Are you feeling okay, sweetie? You look flushed." My mother is sitting across from me drinking her coffee in the exact spot Samuel had me naked and screaming his name two nights ago. I nearly passed out last night when my dad walked into the kitchen and announced *"this is quite the spread"* after Mom and I finished setting the table for dinner. Before we ate, I tried to take a seat in that chair, but she beat me to it. Unfortunately, this morning she's claimed that as her space again.

"I'm fine," I offer with a slight smile.

"Oh, honey, I'm upset that we have to leave early, too." She reaches for my hand across the table and gives me a light squeeze.

I'm flushed because my delivery driver had me naked on this table less than forty-eight hours ago, not because you have to leave early due to a snowstorm.

I keep that internal thought to myself and simply agree with her instead. "I'm glad you guys were able to get a flight for tonight, though; at least the airline allowed you to plan around the storm."

"Me too. We will have a day to recoup before your brother gets to town as well."

"All done." My dad claps his hands together and joins us in the kitchen. "I went ahead and tossed the whole thing in the dumpster. You should really call the moving company and have them replace it. I can't believe they were so careless."

I sip my coffee and cast my eyes down to avoid his gaze. I told my parents that the recliner must have been damaged in the move and broke on me yesterday. After realizing it was too heavy for me to lift by myself, I had to think of a story that was more suitable than the truth when they arrived last night.

"I will call—" Just as I attempt to come up with another lie, there's a knock at the door.

"Oooo, are you expecting company?" my mom perks up, and I frown, shaking my head in response. It's ten o'clock in the morning. I've only recently moved to town, and I don't even know anyone.

"I'll get it." My dad stands and heads to the foyer. I hear the click of the door opening and still at the voice carrying from the space.

I didn't order anything.

"Is that Samuel?" my mother whispers excitedly.

I roll my eyes and stand, joining my father and finding my insanely attractive delivery driver with a huge box propped on a dolly. There is a smaller man behind him dressed in a vest labeled "Driver Helper." I assume he is here to help lift the heavier boxes.

"You already ordered a new recliner?" my dad asks, turning as I approach.

"Um, yeah. I did." Except, upon viewing the box, it isn't a recliner. It's a reading chair that I know costs entirely too much money because it's been on my Wishlist for months. Based on the wink said delivery driver gives behind my father's back, I know *exactly* who bought it.

"Good morning, Samuel!" My mom slides up behind me, and he offers her the same grin that drew me in.

"Good morning, Kimberly." She practically swoons as he continues with his humorous gleam. He knows what he's doing. "I can set this inside for you, sir."

"I've got it." Dad's tone is flat, intentionally making his voice deeper.

"Would you like me to place it here? I've got another package for your daughter." Samuel places the dolly flat on the ground right outside my door.

"What did you just say?" My father's nostrils flare, and I fight back a grin at the insinuation.

"A package." Samuel turns and grabs a much smaller box from the man standing behind him. "For your daughter."

Oh shit. It wasn't an insinuation at all. He really does have another package for me.

I step forward before my dad can puff out his chest any further and accept the box. "Thank you. I forgot I ordered these." I didn't order shit. Upon feeling the weight, I know exactly what's inside, and I glower at him.

"Have a great day," he says with a wave, and returns to his truck with his helper following close behind.

"Bye, Samuel!" Mom calls over my shoulder, and I quickly slam the door shut, hoping he didn't hear her.

"I really think Samuel is a nice boy, Jules. Have you considered asking him out?"

"Mom, just stop. No. I moved here for work, not to seek out eligible bachelors."

"Jules, I'm not getting younger; you really need to settle down. At this rate, I'm going to be on my deathbed by the ti—"

"Stop!" The word leaves my mouth in a furious yell. Even with my mom's face dropping at the outburst, I can't bring myself to feel bad. I know Samuel deliberately ignoring my requests not to replace my things contributes to my ire, and I shouldn't be lashing out at her, but I've endured too long of her constant inquisitions about my love life. I can't take anymore.

"What did you get?" Dad lifts the smaller box in question. He's done this since I was little. When Mom and I argue, instead of stepping in, he always makes attempts to simply change the subject.

"Books." I can't help the annoyance that laces my reply.

"You should've sent me a list. We could have gotten you some for Christmas," Mom replies. She won't make eye contact with me, a strong indicator that I've really upset her.

I close my eyes and take a deep breath. Not wanting them to leave on a bad note, I change trajectories to something Mom and I can bond over. "Would you like to see my dress for the party tomorrow?"

"Oh, yes!" A sparkle returns to her blue eyes, and I'm thankful.

I spend the next hour letting her decide what accessories I should wear and listening to her swoon over the fit of the satin gown. My father seemed less than impressed with the slit up the side, but Mom stepped in and shut him down.

By the time they have to leave for the airport, my mother and I are on much better terms. Although, my frustration with Samuel is still prominent. As soon as the door latches behind them I pull my phone from my pocket and send him a text.

> **I told you not to buy me anything.**

I specifically told him not to replace my ruined things, yet he did it anyway. Why the hell can't people respect me when I say no to something? I have enough mental exhaustion to deal with from my mother's visit; I didn't expect Samuel to add to that stress.

My anger is bubbling up the longer I think about it. Of course, the thought was nice, but we aren't dating. He's not my boyfriend, and now I feel obligated to pay him back. The fact that I have to wait nearly eight hours to finally receive a response gives me too much time to marinate about the situation.

> **I ruined them, it's only right that I replace them.**

> **You explicitly ignored me, it's not your responsibility.**

> **Do you not like the chair?**

> **I can't pay you back for a thousand-dollar fucking chair!!**

> **It's a gift. You don't have to pay me back.**

The fact that he's entirely missing the point pisses me off even more.

> I think we should be done with whatever this is. Didn't your parents teach you how to respect someone's boundaries when they ask you not to fucking do something?

My hands are shaking. From anger or regret? I'm not sure. A small voice in the back of my head is already reprimanding me for ending whatever this is, but we both knew it was only temporary.

> No. My dad is an asshole, and my mother never got the chance. But I guess that's not information for something so casual.

What?

Although my gut tells me exactly what that meant, I still ask for confirmation.

> What do you mean she never got the chance?

After thirty minutes of silence, I finally decide he's not offering me a response; I know I don't deserve one. With a sigh, I type one last text and shut my phone off for the rest of the night.

> I'm sorry.

Chapter 12

Samuel

For someone who owns a multi-million-dollar company, Dad sure went cheap on the liquor for this party. I throw back the rest of my Jack and Coke and head to the bar to retrieve another. There is a gaudy balloon arch over the entrance and at least twelve Christmas trees lining the walls of the large conference room. Remove one of those and he'd have more room in the budget for a nicer bottle of whiskey. Regardless of the lack of top-shelf options, I'll still be drinking my way through the supply tonight.

I've been in a shit mood since the argument with Jules last night. I woke up to an apology text but ultimately left her on read. If I'm going to make it through a night in my father's presence, being inebriated is the best option.

The alcohol in my system does little to take my mind off Jules though. Around this time of night, she's normally texting me to come over. That's all shot to hell now. All because I wanted to be a nice person. *Nice guys finish last, asshole.*

She's right, though; I crossed a clear boundary. The only person I have to be upset with is myself. My glass hits the bar with a little more force than intended. At least I get the bartender's attention for another round, I guess.

"Oooo, someone is broody tonight." The familiar voice behind me has me breathing easier than I have all night and I turn to give my sister a hug.

"Hey, Mo."

She's dressed in a floor-length red sequin gown. Her black hair is pinned up on the side. Looking every bit the part of the CEO's child as I do.

"What's got you in such a pissed-off mood?" she chuckles.

"I don't want to be at this party."

"Cheers to that. At least the alcohol is free. Can't say Dad never did anything for us." She lifts whatever cranberry Christmas cocktail she has and I frown, wondering how long she's been at the party if she already has a drink.

"When did you get here?" I question, retrieving my now full glass from the bartender and taking a sip. I have the urge to ask him for a stronger pour next time but decide against it.

"About twenty minutes ago. I came with CEO Donner himself."

As if she summoned him, Dad's voice greets me next. "Son." His strong hand claps me on the shoulder, and I turn to face him. "Good to see you here."

"You sent a car to my house. I wasn't aware I had a choice," I deadpan.

His eyes narrow in a silent warning before he laughs the comment off as if we are a nice family having an endearing conversation. No doubt a show for his friends and employees. "I'd like to see both of you in my office after this. We need to talk about your positions at the company next quarter."

I look from my dad to Morgan who has the same expression plastered to her face as I do. One that screams *hell no.*

As soon as I open my mouth to argue, Mary, my father's assistant, calls out for everyone's attention over the speakers.

"I have to go make a speech. I will find you two later. Behave," he scolds us like adolescent children and dismisses himself.

"As if we have the option to have fun. This party fucking blows." Morgan pulls the straw from her cocktail and throws back the rest of her drink. "You know, he offered me that one job."

"Head of marketing?" I guess. It's the only position I know of that he had vacant recently.

"Uh-huh." Her eyes remain on our father as he veers through the crowd toward the makeshift stage they've set up at the head of the room.

"Why didn't you take it? We'd see each other more, at least."

She shrugs. "I like Arizona... reminds me of Mom."

We sit in silence for a moment, the mood instantly somber at the mention of our mother. This is why Morgan and I can never drink together. Her motive for staying in Arizona is the exact reason I moved to Canada. I spent most of last night in my head after bringing up Mom to Jules. The subject needs to change before we make this party even more unbearable.

"Let's go mingle. Dad will be pissed if we aren't properly introducing ourselves to his minions." I hold my arm out in a mock-formal gesture.

She laughs, retrieves her fresh drink, stands up straight, and loops her hand around my bicep. "Let's."

Half of the people in attendance aren't even direct employees of the company. If they aren't higher-ups, they're the bankers and CEOs of corporations Dad does business with. I'm the only blue-collar worker in attendance. There are no lower-level employees here; they all get shitty parties at their respective branches.

We don't walk far before spotting one of the few guests I don't mind exchanging conversation with. Ian McCoy, Chief Executive Officer of the Royal Bank of Canada, is standing at one of the cocktail tables closest to us, so Morgan and I visit him first. He has been a family friend since we moved here as children. Upon seeing my sister and I approaching, he faces us with a broad smile. Though he exudes money and power just like my father, Ian is a much more inviting person.

"Samuel! Morgan!" Ian bellows in excitement, gives me a hug, and places a kiss on Morgan's cheek. He grips my biceps and steps back to look at me. "Did you get taller?"

He's made this same joke every time he's seen me since I was thirteen, and I always respond with a laugh.

We get very little conversation in before the clinking of glass interrupts us, and my father's voice sounds over the speakers. The room goes silent. Welcoming his attendees first, he follows by announcing the introduction of his newest head of marketing. A position I wish my sister had taken. My interest is waning, so I mindlessly trace the rim of my glass.

"Miss Harrington, if you could please join me on stage?"

I flip my head at the familiar name, and my eyes widen as I watch her accept the microphone from my father.

Chapter 13

Jules

I've been nursing the same glass of champagne since I arrived fifteen minutes ago. The shadows in this corner of the room have done well to mask me from the partygoers. I'm not exactly in the mood to mingle, and from what I've seen, there are very few people I recognize in the dim lighting, anyway. I haven't taken the time to observe all of them. I can't summon the interest. For what seems like the thousandth time since last night, my thoughts lock on my argument with Samuel.

I spent the majority of the evening convincing myself that *she never got the chance*' could mean hundreds of things so that I wouldn't feel like a complete asshole. Maybe she ran off with the hot pool boy and decided to travel the world, or...

"I don't believe we've met," a deep voice startles me, and I spin around, taking in the tall, clean-shaven man. Thousands of Christmas lights line the ceiling, giving the room a dim glow that reflects in his blue eyes and darkens his features. He's attractive, but not in a Samuel sort of way.

Fucking hell, stop.

"We haven't, I'm new to the company." My response is less than cheerful. The last thing I want to do is give this guy the wrong impression. I ended my situationship with my delivery driver last night. Now isn't exactly a great time to start an office romance. Even if he does look like the kind of guy my mother would approve of. *She approved of Samuel too, dumbass.*

I roll my eyes at my internal reprimanding.

"I'm sorry, did I offend you?"

"Oh, no," I sputter. "Sorry, Jules Harrington." I offer him my hand.

"Matthew Sharp. CEO of Sharp Industries." He introduces himself as if I'm supposed to know exactly what company that is and accepts my outstretched hand. Only, instead of a shake, he places a kiss on the back. I pull away from him, and he slides closer, brushing his fingers along the exposed skin of my back. A shudder races through me at the gesture. "So, Jules. Why haven't we met?"

I don't want to make small talk with this man, and I especially don't want him touching me. I step back and drink down the champagne I'd sworn off before my introduction. My eyes scan the room for a waiter, needing a reason to put distance between myself and Matthew. Instead, I hear the clinking of glass, and Mr. Donner calling for the attention of his guests.

"Good evening, everyone. I'm so grateful you were all able to join us for the annual Donner Logging Christmas Eve party. After another record-breaking year, I'm elated to celebrate the holiday season and offer you all a much-needed break. When my late wife and I started this company, I never imagined that we would be the empire we are today. Donner is the leader in the logging industry, and that's all thanks to you."

I've only known Alexander Donner a short time; he's always seemed like a broody asshole of a man who runs his empire with an iron fist. Hearing him address those he works with now, he exudes anything but.

"Before our festivities, I'd like to introduce you all to our newest head of marketing. Miss Harrington, if you could please join me on stage?" His eyes scan the room before landing on mine.

I happily escape CEO Sharp and weave through the slew of people surrounding the cocktail tables, making my way to join him in the brightest section of the room. Already missing my hiding spot in the shadows before the unwelcome interruption. The smile he offers me reaches his familiar brown eyes, and my heart hitches a bit as it reminds me of Samuel. I shake away the thought. Is this really going to happen every time I see someone with eyes the same dark shade? *Stop thinking about him!*

The guests all clap in greeting and my face heats. I can stand in front of a boardroom and give presentations all day long. Ask me to talk to random people at a company party? Not my idea of a good time.

When I reach the risers arranged into a stage, he shakes my hand and hands me the microphone. "Thank you, Mr. Donner."

I face the crowd. "I'm excited to be part of the Donner Logging team." My eyes move around the room, making sure to focus on anyone but the handsy man in the back. I stop when my gaze lands on a face I recognize at the front, staring back at me with wide eyes. The gorgeous raven-haired woman beside him grips his arm as she leans in and whispers something in his ear with a grin. "I... Sorry... I. Thank you for the opportunity." I say abruptly and rush off the stage.

Why the fuck is he here?

Chapter 14

Samuel

"Oh, she's cute," Morgan whispers and grips my bicep to get my attention. I can hear the grin in her voice, but I can't take my eyes off Jules. She's not cute, she's *fucking stunning*. Adorned in a forest-green satin dress that perfectly hugs every curve. My eyes fall to the slit that nearly reaches her hip, and I ball my fists as I try to get my thoughts in order.

She's Donner Logging's newest employee? *How the fuck did this happen?*

She stammers when her bright blue eyes meet my gaze, and then she's darting off the stage. Without a second thought, I leave the table I'd been occupying, and race to catch up to her before she makes it to the exit. She's trying to leave. To my relief, she keeps getting stopped by guests congratulating her on the new position. I'm grateful because it buys me time to get across the room. Her pace slows as she offers half smiles and thank yous. She spots me close behind and abandons all pleasantries in a rush to the doors.

When she reaches the hallway, she quickens her escape. I lengthen my strides and follow her all the way to the elevator. The doors slide open, and the moment she's inside, she frantically presses the button to close them. But I'm already there, throwing my hand out and stepping in with her.

"Get out," she hisses.

I ignore her, and the doors slide shut. "Why didn't you tell me *this* was the job you took?"

She reaches around me and presses the button for the main level. "That's not information you had any right to know." She crosses her arms over her chest. "Why don't you go back to the party? Your girlfriend is waiting for you, I'm sure."

Girlfriend? I can't help the laugh that escapes me when I piece together that she must mean Morgan. "Is that what this is about?" I close in on her space until her back is against the wall and place my hand above her head.

Her breath hitches, and for a moment, all I can think about is fucking her right here in this elevator. Though I doubt her misplaced anger will have her up for that, and I only have eight more floors to explain myself. Staring down my nose, I release a chuckle void of humor. "You jealous, Jules?" I've waited weeks for her to admit that our connection is more than just late-night sex.

She shoves me hard, but I don't budge. "No. I just don't make a habit of sleeping with taken men."

"I'm not taken," I state simply.

She barks a sarcastic scoff, and her eyes narrow on me. "Then why the fuck are you at *my* company's Christmas party if you're not here with her?"

"You mean, my *father's* Christmas party that I came to with my *sister*?"

"Sister?" She pauses. Thinking that over for a brief moment before her ire returns. "Bullshit. You're a fucking delivery driver."

I've had plenty of women show interest in me because of my namesake. Which is why I didn't mind keeping things casual with minimal talk of our personal lives. Her questioning my integrity because I enjoy my job as a courier frustrates the hell out of me, though. If she wants proof, I'll give it to her.

The elevator dings and the doors slide open. Jules moves to get around me, but I catch her arm, push her back against the wall, and close them again before pressing the button to take us to the thirty-fifth floor. The action reminds me of the last time I was at her apartment, and my eyes trail down her body at the thought. The smooth skin of her leg is on display through the slit in her dress, leaving my hands aching to touch her. My cock simultaneously twitches at the thought of fisting those pretty blonde curls framing her face.

Not the fucking time, Samuel. A low growl releases from my throat as I fight with my own conscience to use words, and not my dick, to show her who I really am. I sigh in frustration.

"Next time you spend several weeks in a casual relationship with someone, maybe consider asking their last name at some point." I never gave her information because she never asked. She's been too damn adamant that we not make this more than what it is... *was.*

She shakes her head. "You're lying. You're not Mr. Donner's son. And it's not like you asked for my full name either."

"I deliver your packages, *Jules Harrington*. I already *know* your name." I purposefully ignore her accusation that I'm being dishonest. She'll know the truth soon enough.

"Let me out." The protest is feeble as her eyes drop to my mouth.

"I will once I clear my name. I don't enjoy being called a liar, sweetheart." My lips are mere centimeters from hers, and I can't take it, even knowing she ended things. There is an electricity between us that always pulls me toward her. The forced proximity makes the need unbearable, and our mouths collide.

I'm not soft with her, and she returns the sentiment as her hands grip my hair. Both of us releasing the frustration of the last twenty-four hours with a searing kiss. She moans into my mouth, the sound pure ecstasy. I reach down, grab the back of her thigh, and hook it around my hip. Needing her closer, I trail my hand up until I'm gripping her ass, pressing my hard cock against her center and realizing she's bare.

"Why the hell aren't you wearing underwear?"

"I didn't want lines in my dress," she breathes.

With a low groan, I ball my hand into a fist above her. Silently begging myself to think with the right head. Between her perfect ass in my hand and her doe eyes pleading for me to take her right here, I'm about to break what little resolve I'm grasping onto.

The elevator dings, signaling that we've made it to the top floor. Dropping her leg, I push myself from the wall, and walk straight out the door.

Chapter 15

Jules

I pause, my lips aching from how forcefully Samuel kissed me. The momentary lapse in judgment rooting me to the spot. Samuel retreats from the elevator as if nothing has happened. He doesn't ask me to follow, and I briefly question if I should. The doors begin closing, and curiosity gets the better of me. I quickly step out into the reception area, my heels clicking against the tile, resounding through the empty space. The silence is eerie. I've never been to the executive level at night. Everyone who works on this floor is enjoying the party downstairs.

Samuel takes purposeful strides until he is standing in front of the familiar dark, mahogany door labeled *Alexander Donner, Chief Executive Officer*—the office where I meet with Mr. Donner every week. Samuel pulls a keycard from the pocket of his suit and swipes it over the scanner. When the lock clicks open, my stomach drops.

He turns to face me, holding the card between his fingers and proving that a picture of him alongside his name is printed on it. "Hi, Miss Harrington, I'm Samuel Donner. Son of the Chief Executive Officer of Donner Logging Company. Or, as you so eloquently pointed out, *just a fucking delivery driver.*'" The sarcasm in his exclamation furthers the guilt I'm feeling, and my eyes fall to the floor.

Suddenly, the connection hits me like a freight train.

She never got the chance...

"My late wife"...

"Samuel, I... I'm sorry," I whisper. Not able to make eye contact with him. For the second time in the last twenty-four hours, I've put my foot in my mouth.

He grabs my hand and forcefully pulls me into the office before slamming the door behind us and pushing me against it. My heart rate picks up. This is the office of the CEO. My employer. I'm not supposed to be here.

"I don't want your apology. I want you to tell me why you got so mad," he says, pulling me flush against his chest. His earthy scent makes me heady, and I'm thrown into memories of the last three weeks with his body pressed to mine in this way.

I can't focus with his proximity of him so I remove myself from his arms and walk across the room to stand before the floor-to-ceiling windows. The snow is falling much heavier now. "I didn't know you were my boss' son." It's not a lie, but it's not the truth he's looking for.

He meets me at the windows and grips my shoulders, dropping his mouth to my ear. The stubble of his beard skates along my jawline, eliciting goosebumps down my arms, and making the hair on the back of my neck stand up. "Cute. Now tell me the truth."

"Because I…" *Am I really about to admit that I'm a jealous bitch who can't handle seeing him with someone else?*

"Because you what?" He trails his fingers down my spine and along the exposed skin of my back. I can't deny how responsive I am to his touch.

Fuck it. I want him.

I lift my chin and turn to look at him. The city's lights thirty-five floors below us shadow his features, giving new meaning to my darkest desires. "I don't want you with anyone else, Samuel."

"About damn time," he growls.

As soon as the words leave his mouth, my front is pushed against the wall of windows overlooking the city. Instinctively, my hands find purchase on the glass, and I swallow hard as he sweeps my hair around the side of my shoulder. The feel of his fingers brushing my skin has my heart racing in anticipation.

"Now, your *boss' son* is going to claim you so thoroughly that you won't be able to sit in this room without thinking of me. I may not want my father's company, but every time you meet with him, I want you to remember *exactly* who I am." The sound of his voice is amplified by the adrenaline coursing through me. His breath skates along my neck, creating a layer of condensation on the window as he leans in closer. "I'm really going to enjoy fucking you in front of all of Calgary, sweetheart."

The extra inches from my heels line us up perfectly, and I grind my ass against him in response, mimicking the last time he had me in this position. I can feel how hard he is through the fabric separating us. "Fuck, Jules," he breathes. My thighs clench in response to his words. If I were wearing underwear, they'd be soaked.

His hand drops to my thigh and disappears beneath the slit of my dress. When he reaches my center, his fingers circle my clit. I moan in response, closing my eyes and lolling my forehead forward to rest on the glass. Instinctively, my legs spread wider for him; an invitation he accepts willingly. Two fingers enter me, and he continues the agonizingly sweet torment.

"Always so fucking wet for me," he praises. His free hand begins removing the sleeves of my dress, and I pull my arms through the satin. The top half pools around my waist, leaving me bare. He nudges me forward, and the sensation of the cold glass on my breasts sends me into a frenzy. Even with the distance between the window and the street lights below, the rush of being seen mixed with the rhythm of his fingers is all too much, and I'm already on the brink of orgasm.

Just before the dam bursts, he removes his fingers. I release a whimper, and he flips me around to face him. A dark chuckle accompanies the devilish gleam in his eyes. "Not yet, sweetheart." He denies me as he brings his hand to my lips. I part them, and he presses his fingers into my mouth. As the taste of my arousal hits my tongue, his deep brown eyes flare with excitement. "See how good you taste? You're a fucking drug, Jules."

My entire body heats with his words and I know I'm done for. "More. Please, Samuel," I plead. I'm half naked, pressed against the glass pane that overlooks the whole of Calgary, in the office of the man who runs the empire of the logging industry, begging his son to fuck me, and I can't find it in me to care. Samuel has managed to infiltrate every last coherent thought I have and I can't think of anything else but finally allowing myself to be his fully.

Giving into my plea, Samuel reaches down and unties the knot around my waist. Forest-green satin falls to the floor, and he follows. The second his knees hit the carpet, his mouth is on my pussy. He brings my knee up to rest on his shoulder, sucks my clit into his mouth, and begins flicking his tongue. The grazing of his teeth against me has another orgasm building. I grip his shoulders as I grind against his mouth. He turns his head and places a sharp bite to the inside of my thigh, causing me to cry out.

Marking his territory.

Every time we have sex, he marks me. Only now do I understand that this is his way of claiming me. And only now do I allow myself to realize how fucking hot that is.

He inserts his fingers inside me once again, his mouth still tormenting my clit, and within seconds, ecstasy explodes through every fiber of my being. He continues pumping his fingers through every last moment of my orgasm.

When I finally catch my breath, I look down to meet his gaze.

"Don't worry, sweetheart. I'm not done with you yet." He grins and points to Mr. Donner's desk in the center of the room.

Chapter 16

Samuel

"Put your hands on the desk," I command, but she doesn't move.

"What about your fath—"

"Jules, you're already naked in his office. It's a little late to be concerned about my father. Turn. Around."

Her face heats as she concedes and walks forward, placing her palms on either side of his name plaque. I can't help the devilish grin that splits my face at what is about to happen. Fucking her on my dad's desk wasn't exactly my intention. Though, neither was seeing her at the party. He will be able to see that my keycard accessed his office tonight, and with her bent over his desk for me, there isn't a part of me that gives a fuck.

I unlatch my belt and free my throbbing cock from the confines of my pants. Lining myself up with her center, I reach forward and wrap her long blonde curls around my fist. I'll never tire of seeing her at my mercy like this. I grip my cock and slowly slide the tip up and down her entrance in a teasing motion.

"Please... Samuel..." Her head rolls back as she moans my name; the sound is fucking addicting. I slam into her, causing her to cry out once more.

Hard slaps resound around the room as I fuck her. I'm not gentle with her; she's never asked me to be. "Fucking addicting, Jules," I hiss through clenched teeth as I feel her tightening around my cock. My hand connects with her ass with a crack, and she yelps as I continue the punishing thrusts. I can already tell she's close, her cries of pleasure urging me on. I release her hair and grip her waist with both hands, giving me more leverage.

"More," she begs, and with that I pull out of her. I spin her around and shove her back down on the cherrywood.

She lays back and wraps her legs around me. I watch as I slide my cock back into her pussy. Giving myself time to appreciate the view, I slowly stroke in and out of her, loving the way she takes every inch of me so well.

"Good girl," I praise, before I grip her hips again and continue right where we left off. Only this time, my gaze trails between her breasts bouncing with the force of my thrusts, and my slick cock sliding in and out of her. I place a hand on the desk and lean further over her, the position allowing me to hit deeper. "Now, come for me."

Her fingernails dig into my forearms as she ignites at my words. I silence her screams in a bruising kiss and, with a few last pumps, spiral into succession. Filling her completely.

We work to catch our breath. After a few minutes, Jules groans, throwing her arm over her face. "I have to quit my job."

I laugh and pull her up to stand with me. "Don't worry about your job. I'll make sure Dad doesn't know you were up here with me."

"Samuel. I cannot sit in that chair and make eye contact with the man ever again!" she exclaims.

"You'll sit in that chair every week and be reminded of what you have waiting for you."

"What?" Her brows furrow.

"You're mine now, Jules, as much as I'm yours." I place a kiss on her forehead. This time, she doesn't recoil. Instead, she wraps her hands around my neck and kisses me.

"I'm yours, Samuel," she confirms.

A wide smile splits my face, and I brush a stray lock of hair behind her ear. "Let's get dressed."

While I dress, she walks to the window to retrieve her gown. I hate every part of the satin that begins covering her once more, wishing we could spend the night together. Alas, there is still a party happening downstairs that we should probably get back to. I pull my phone from my pocket to text my sister and ask if Dad is looking for me yet. My thumbs begin typing but I'm stopped in my tracks when the telling sound of a keycard beeps outside the door. My eyes snap up to Jules who is staring at me in horror and rushing to shove her arms through the sleeves of her dress.

I wrack my brain for any excuse I can give my father. But considering there are very distinct handprints on the window I just had Jules pinned to, I'm falling short.

My shoulders slump in relief when Morgan walks through the door. Stopping in the threshold, her wide eyes flip from me to Jules, and I quickly try to find an excuse that won't mortify Jules. "Miss

Harrington and I were just discussing the position I might take at the company next quarter. I was going to ask dad about managing the branch closest to Coals Lake."

Morgan barks a laugh and points to the handprints on the window. "I have no doubt you were discussing *positions* with *Miss Harrington.*"

Fair. That was a shit lie. My sister knows there is no way in hell I'm working here. I'll just give our father the runaround until we are in the same spot next year. With a groan, I run a hand down my face before pulling my tie from my pocket. Jules is rooted to the spot. The moonlight bright enough to tell me that her face has gone crimson. I stride across the room to join her by the window. Changing trajectories as I use the fabric in my hand to clean the handprints from the window.

"Jules." My hand rests on the small of her back. "This is Morgan. My sister."

Jules' eyes widen, and the guilt she felt earlier returns. Clearing her throat, she gives a small wave. "It's nice to meet you."

"Likewise." Morgan winks at her. Grinning in humor, she's not helping the situation in the slightest.

"Why are *you* up here, Mo?"

"You left and that party is unbearable. I know dad keeps better liquor up here. Figured I'd sit and drink before he summoned us." She shrugs and walks to the cabinet on the far side of the room that houses the crystal decanter filled with expensive whiskey. "Glad to see you had the same idea."

I ignore her antics and lower my voice while speaking to Jules. "We should leave. Come back to my room with me." I grab her hand and give a light squeeze. Hoping I haven't run out of Christmas miracles just yet.

She looks around my shoulder to my sister. I follow her line of sight to where Morgan is now perched in my dad's chair with a glass in her hand, and bare feet crossed on the top of his desk. "One; I can hear you. Two; go. I'll tell dad you got sick or something."

I know Dad won't believe that for a second, I'll end up with a phone call first thing tomorrow. But he'll get over it... eventually. Right now, all I care about is Jules, and the fact that she looks like she wants to be anywhere but this office. The tension rolling off of her is palpable. I grab her shoulders and bring her focus back to me. "I will get a rideshare, and we can go back to the hotel. Spend the night with me?" My heart beats in anticipation as I wait for her answer. She's made her stance on overnight stays very clear in the past, but tonight I'm hoping things have changed.

Her blue eyes gleam, and she nods. "Okay, let's go."

I smile back at my sister as I take Jules's hand in mine. "Thanks, Mo. I owe you one."

Morgan lifts her glass in mock salutation. "Damn right you do." She takes another sip of her drink, and Jules and I disappear through the door.

For the first time in a long time, I'm excited to wake up on Christmas morning.

Chapter 17

Jules

New Years Eve

"It's 11:59!" I'm met with a faraway "dammit" and the sound of footsteps on the hardwood. *Is he running?*

Confirming my suspicion, Samuel bursts into the living room a little too quickly, and his foot catches on the rug. Popcorn goes flying, and the man falls to the floor with a hard *thump*.

"Oh, shit." I jump from the couch and hurry over to him. "Are you okay?"

"Kiss me!"

Standing above him, my face twists in confusion. The man just busted his ass on my hardwood and is now requesting a kiss?

He sits up, grabs my hand, and yanks me to the floor to straddle him just as the alarm on his phone starts blaring. My head spins from the buzz of champagne in my system, accompanied by the haste he pulled me down in, and I can't help but laugh. "Did you set an alarm for midnight?"

"Yes, I didn't want to miss it." He silences the alarm and looks back at me. His dark eyes light up as his hand laces through my hair, and he pulls me into a searing kiss. I loop my arms around his neck and melt into him.

The last week has been pure bliss since admitting I felt more for him than I had let on. Every time he's kissed me it's been with passion and deeper meaning. I still find myself reverting back to the terrified feelings of commitment, but Samuel has shown nothing but understanding.

I pull back and smile at him. "You didn't have to physically injure yourself to kiss me at midnight."

"I'm not injured; I'm just fine." His hands creep beneath the hem of my shirt, and heat pools in my belly when he kisses my neck. "And the kiss is for good luck."

"You don't need luck, Samuel. You've already got me." I chuckle, softening under his touch, the rough skin of his hands warm against my sides.

"Remember that... because I have something to tell you." He grips me tighter as if I'll disappear, and the aura in the room completely shifts. My stomach drops. I'm not ready for this. I may have given myself to him exclusively, but I'm nowhere near a point for him to drop the "L" word on me.

With my heart beating to a frantic rhythm and anxiety quickly taking over, I rush to stop him before he can continue. "Samuel, don—"

"No," he cuts me off. "I know I ruined the signed copies of your books."

I sigh in relief and place a hand on my chest. "Oh, thank goodness." I chuckle. "I thought you were going to say you loved me." *Shit.* I curse my alcohol-infused state for voicing what should have stayed internal.

"What? Of course I don't."

My eyes widen at how quickly that response comes out. I don't want the man to be in love with me... but damn.

"Wait, no. Shit. That sounds bad; I mean... I just—" He shakes his head in exasperation and drops his head into his hand.

I pull his fingers from over his eyes so he's looking at me when I laugh. "That's reassuring. Also, I don't care that my books are ruined."

The man is in a full-on state of confusion, and I can't blame him. I'm a hot mess. Still, he seems relieved to change the subject back to his original point. "I know, but I still feel responsible." Shifting me so that he can reach for his phone, he pulls up an email. "Don't get mad, but I got you tickets to a signing in February."

He what? My eyes widen when he shows me the confirmation. *That signing is sold out.*

My mouth is agape as I sit in silence. When his face drops, I can see the worry in Samuel's eyes. *"Don't get mad,"* I repeat his words in my head and realize he thinks I'm going to leave again after what happened when he gifted me the recliner.

"Thank you, Samuel. You're extremely thoughtful." My hand caresses his face, reassuring him that I'm not running this time, and I lean down to kiss him. I feel the tension release from his body the moment our lips meet, and he uses his grip on my waist to pull me further into him.

"You're worth it," he murmurs against my lips, and I squeal as he quickly flips me over so that he's on top. His head turns as he looks at the mess he made and frowns. "I wanted to eat the popcorn, but I guess you'll have to do."

I giggle and playfully slap his chest. "You're an insatiable man, ya know that?"

"Only for you, sweetheart." He winks and scoops me off the floor, carrying me to the couch, where I curl into his chest.

"Happy New Year, Jules," he murmurs.

A contented smile crosses my face as I feel the soft press of his lips on the top of my head. "Happy New Year, Samuel."

May it be the best one yet.

Acknowledgments

To my street team—my favorite readers, and the sweetest humans—I hope this was everything you needed in an emotional reprieve. Thank you for all you do, for being so patient with me this year, and for continuously being the most supportive group. I've told you before, and I'll continue to let you know, I have so much gratitude for you.

To Katie, my editor, my friend, and one of the most genuinely beautiful humans I have ever known. Thank you for the hard work you put into this book. I know I can be a lot to work with, and you always take my antics in stride. I can't wait for all our future projects together.

Last but not least, to Julie, thank you for being so grumpy. Love you forever.

Let's Stay Connected!

TikTok – @elizaanneauthor

Instagram – @elizaanneauthor

Facebook – Eliza Anne's Readers

Goodreads – Eliza Anne

Website – elizaanneauthor.com

Email – authorelizaanne@gmail.com